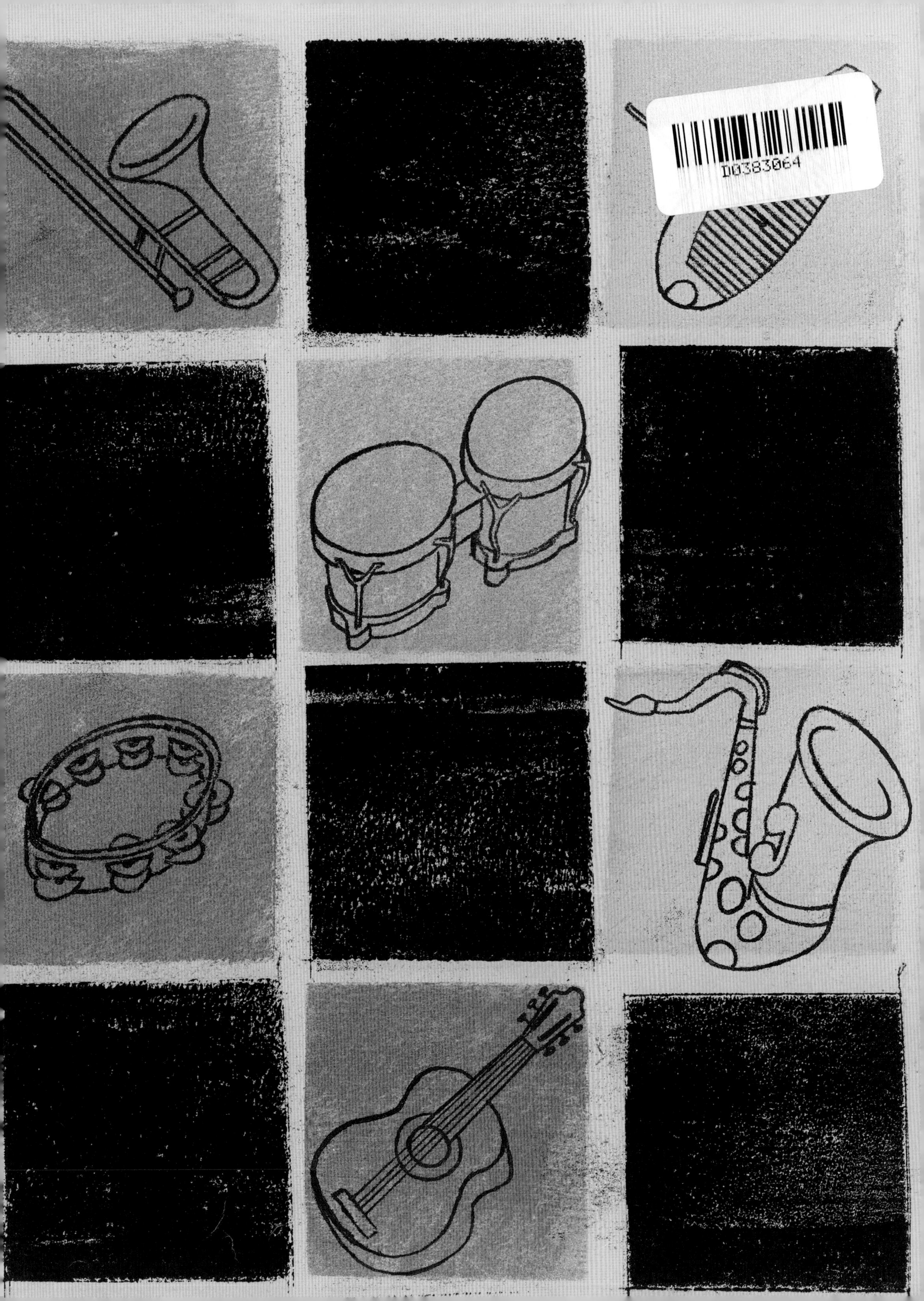
D0383064

To Sugely Chaidez, Mercedes Parodi, and my parents—
each of whom taught me very necessary first steps

—K. S.

For Jennifer and Sofia

Special thanks to my model, Olivia Blanco, and her family

—E. R.

Henry Holt and Company, LLC, *Publishers since 1866*
175 Fifth Avenue, New York, New York 10010
www.henryholtchildrensbooks.com

Distributed in Canada by H. B. Fenn and Company Ltd.

Library of Congress Cataloging-in-Publication Data
Sciurba, Katie.
Oye, Celia! / Katie Sciurba; illustrated by Edel Rodriguez.—1st ed.
p. cm.
Summary: Illustrations and rhythmic text celebrate the life and music of singer Celia Cruz, as a young fan attends a neighborhood dance party and hears loss, happiness, Latin American culture, and more in her voice and lyrics. Includes translations of Spanish words used.
ISBN-13: 978-0-8050-7468-0 / ISBN-10: 0-8050-7468-6
1. Cruz, Celia—Juvenile fiction. [1. Cruz, Celia—Fiction. 2. Singers—Fiction.
3. Latin Americans—Fiction.] I. Rodriguez, Edel, ill. II. Title.
PZ7.S412750ye 2007 [E]—dc22 2006009233

The artist used pastel, acrylic, spray paint, and oil-based ink on paper
to create the illustrations for this book.
First Edition—2007 / Designed by Laurent Linn
Printed in the United States of America on acid-free paper. ∞
1 3 5 7 9 10 8 6 4 2

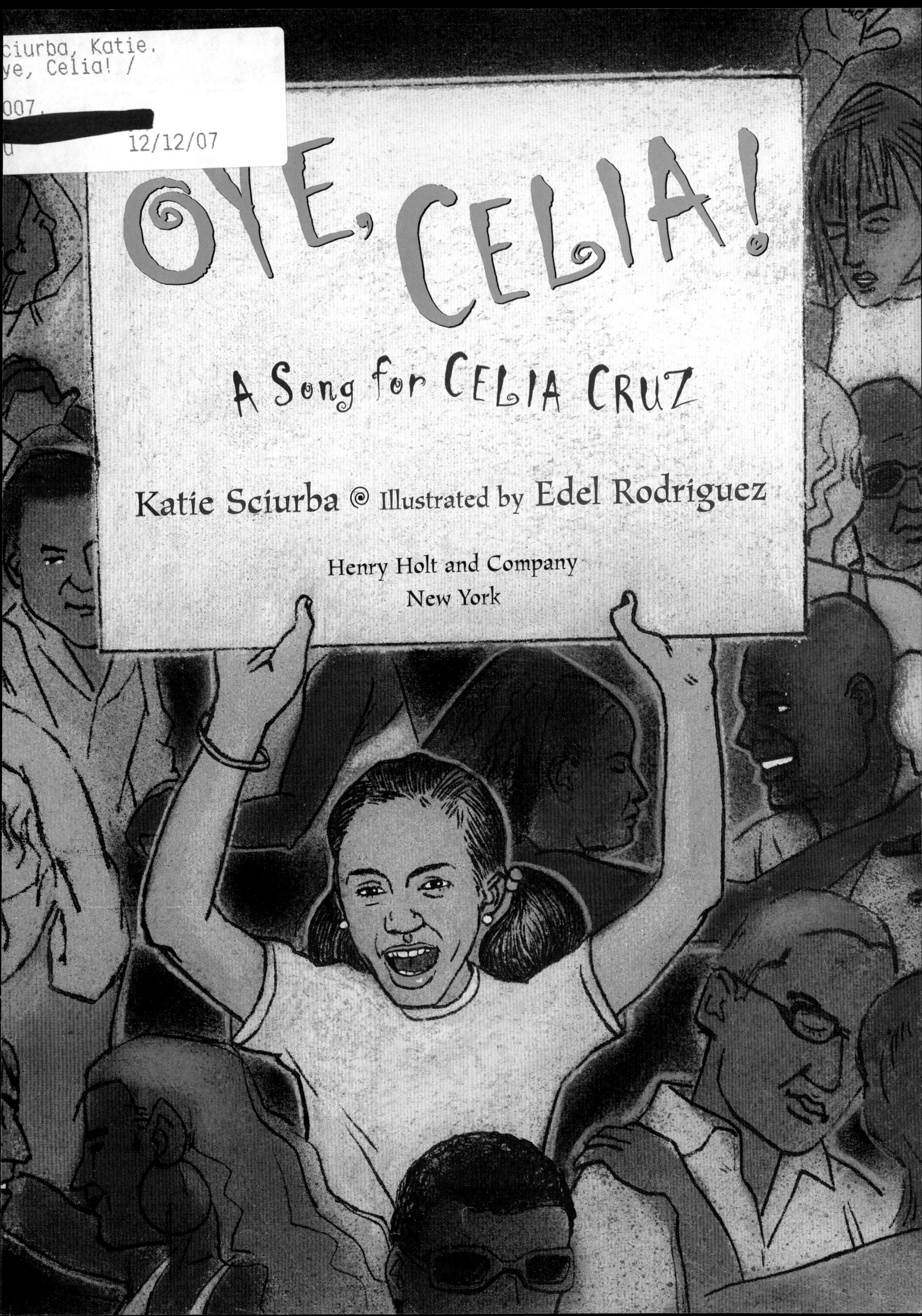
OYE, CELIA!
A Song for CELIA CRUZ
Katie Sciurba @ Illustrated by Edel Rodriguez
Henry Holt and Company
New York

Oye, Celia!

When I hear you, I hear Cuba—
Your Cuba, my Cuba,
Our Cuba.

Your voice pulsates with
The *doong-doong-doong* of the *tambor*,
The *chaka-chaka chaka-chaka* of maracas,
And the *stroom stroom stroom* of the guitar.

My heart beats along.

Celia Cruz,
When I hear you, I hear *la gente*—
Your people, my people,
Our people.

You sing to us, for us, in Spanish—
The language of Cuba, Puerto Rico, Mexico, Ecuador . . .
But even people who don't understand the words
Understand the passion.

I understand the words
and the passion.

Nuestra Celia,
When I hear you, I hear *la tristeza*—
Your sadness, my sadness,
Our sadness.

You tell about your home—
The land you left behind,
The people you will always love,
The country you will never forget.

Sometimes I cry, too.

Unforgettable Celia,
When I hear you, I hear *la historia*—
Your history, my history,
Our history.

Your lyrics breathe life into our ancestors—
Slaves who gathered in stolen moments
To create a rhythm
That was passed down to us.

I thank them.

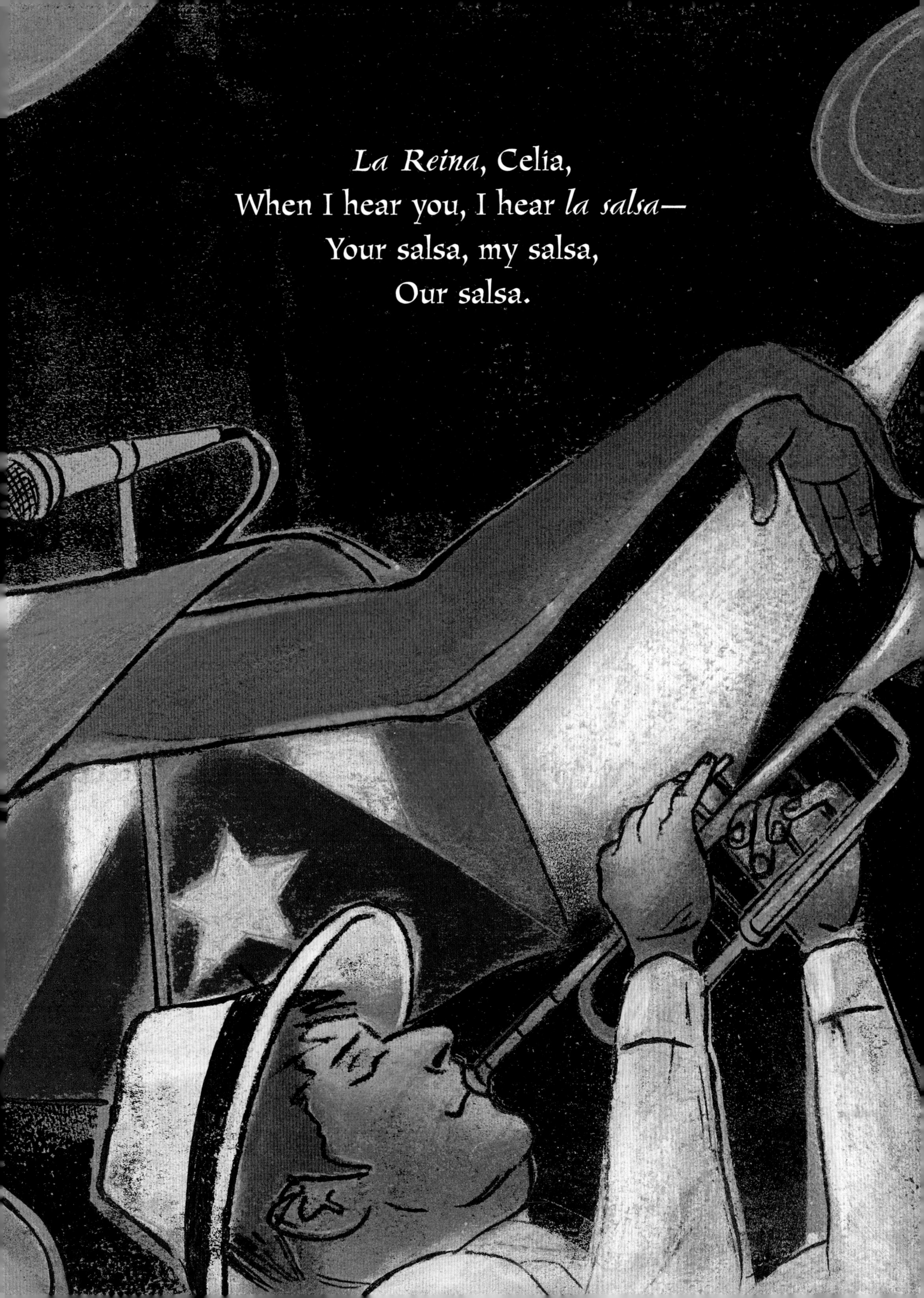

La Reina, Celia,
When I hear you, I hear *la salsa*—
Your salsa, my salsa,
Our salsa.

You mix

“AZÚCAR!”

into the sounds of
Rumba, jazz, *flamenco*, hip-hop, and *guaguancó*.
It becomes a blend, a *salsa*, just like us—
—African, Caribbean, and European.

I am *la salsa*.

Smiling Celia,
When I hear you, I hear *la alegría*—
Your happiness, my happiness,
Our happiness.

Celia

Each of your songs is a *carnaval*
that makes people
dance away their troubles
and celebrate their blessings.

My feet *have* to move
When I hear you,
Celia Cruz.

SPANISH WORDS USED

la alegría (la ah-leh-*gree*-ah). Happiness.

azúcar (ah-*soo*-cahr). Sugar. Celia Cruz was known for shouting this out in the middle of her songs. It began as a story she told about a Cuban waiter who offered her sugar with her coffee. Celia, thinking he was crazy because Cuban coffee *always* comes with sugar, began shouting, "*Azúcar! Azúcar! Azúcar!*" Audiences loved hearing Celia tell this story, but she grew tired of reciting it over and over and over. Later, she just said "*Azúcar!*" and the crowds went wild.

carnaval (car-nah-*vahl*). Carnival.

el cielo (el see-*ell*-oh). Sky or heaven.

flamenco (flah-*mehn*-co). Music characterized by guitar playing and a rhythmic clapping of hands known as *toque de palmas*. Often accompanied by *cantes*, singing that is attributed to the gypsy people.

la gente (la *hen*-tay). People.

guaguancó (wah-wahn-*co*). One of the most popular styles of *rumba* with a fast tempo. In *guaguancó*, the singer must improvise (make up words and sounds) to accompany the music. Celia Cruz was known to improvise for up to twenty minutes at a time.

la historia (la ees-*tor*-ee-ah). History.

nuestra (noo-*es*-trah). Our.

oye (*oh*-yay). Literally, listen. A word often called out in Latin music, particularly *salsa*, to catch the listener's attention.

la reina (la *ray*-nah). The queen. Celia Cruz is known as *la Reina de la Salsa* (Queen of Salsa). She immigrated to the United States from Cuba in 1960 and helped sensationalize Latin music with the legendary band La Sonora Matancera and the musicians Tito Puente and Johnny Pacheco.

rumba (*room*-bah). A type of dance most closely linked to the African slaves brought to Cuba. The rhythm and steps are demonstrations of African religious rituals, which began in slave compounds on Sundays, the only day of the week slaves were allowed a small amount of free time.

la salsa (la *sahl*-sah). Literally, the sauce. A mix of several kinds of music, including pop, jazz, *son*, *rumba*, *guaguancó*, *flamenco*, and Puerto Rican *plenas*, *salsa* is one of today's most popular types of Latin music.

tambor (tahm-*bor*). Drum.

la tristeza (la trees-*tes*-ah). Sadness.

AUTHOR'S NOTE

It was August 2002, and Celia Cruz was about to begin a Central Park Summer Stage performance. I stood amidst thousands of fans whose clapping hands echoed the band's rhythm as the smiling *Reina de la Salsa* danced up to the microphone. Her sequined jacket seemed to reflect the glimmer in our hearts as she belted out her first *"Azúcar!"*

I clutched the original draft of this book in my hand, wishing it was possible for her to read it. Her voice spoke to all of us—the one collective *gente* that adored her. It was easy to feel inspired by Celia Cruz.

Hail began to pelt down on us. But we remained there—standing, dancing, and singing along—until she sang her very last note.

Celia Cruz died in July 2003. It is my hope that this message, *Oye, Celia*, reaches her in *el cielo*.

ILLUSTRATOR'S NOTE

I was introduced to the music of Celia Cruz by my father when I was a child growing up in a small Cuban town in the 1970s. His modest collection of LPs was our main source of entertainment. Friends and family would gather around our living room often, dancing to Celia's music until late in the evening. When we immigrated to Miami, Celia became one of my family's heroes, an example that with hard work, any Cuban could achieve wonderful things in America. Whenever I saw her in concert, her soulful music and dance moves always carried me to our small living room again, to the family and friends we had left behind. When she joyously yelled out "Azúcar," it put my mind right back in the fields I played in, laughing and eating sugarcane with all of my friends.

Celia, I will forever be thankful to you for making music that brings me closer to something I felt I had lost forever.